Between the Stone

Also in this series:

Poetry
- Belongings
- The Legend of Sidora
- No Means No

Prose
- Song of the Arrow
- Tales from Happy Valley
- A Parting Shot
- The Taste of Rain

Drama
- The Coiner's Wife
- Narrowboat Blues
- Denial

For more information, go to www.linguabooks.com

Between the Stone

Poetry and Prose Carved from the
Upper Calder Valley

Alison Milner

www.linguabooks.com

Paperback edition: ISBN 978-1-916511-06-4
eBook edition: ISBN 978-1-916511-07-1

First edition

Editor: Ann Claypole

A CIP catalogue record for this book is available from the British Library.

LinguaBooks
Elsie Whiteley Innovation Centre
Hopwood Lane
Halifax HX1 5ER
www.linguabooks.com

When I began to listen to poetry I began to listen to the stones, and I began to listen to what the clouds had to say, and I began to listen to others. Then you begin to listen to the soul, the soul of yourself which is also the soul of everyone else.

— Joy Harjo

To Michael,

thank you

Preface

Between the breathing of millstone, the grinding of ice, the gouging of water and the rasping of gravel, a dramatic landscape was sculpted in the Upper Calder Valley. The deep wooded ravines and racing becks were harnessed to power a revolution in cloth production. Mill chimneys were thrown up taller than the ancient trees. Wild moorlands of glistening peat and the rocky outcrops remained untamed. Worlds of folklore and myth where boulders speak, and stories are woven, layer the sediment of our lives. The poetry and prose in my book has been excavated from this tradition.

Maybe you will rest on a corpseway by a stay-hither stone and browse awhile through it. Or warm your feet and your imagination by reading these pages beside a roaring fire.

Apart from 'Migration' which won the inaugural Togetherness Poetry Prize and 'Haworth Moor,' part of the 'Sleeping in Frozen Quiet' anthology, none of the poetry and prose in this book has previously been published.

Contents

Part One - A Spinning of Leaves

Words

I keep my words
in a gilded cage
songbirds singing
an opera of emotion
with ambiguous meaning.
I do not release them
give them wings to fly
feathering the sky
with cloudy thoughts
or permit their webbed feet
to wade in the shallows.
I scatter them on an ebb tide
like the ashes of the dead.

Following the Heron Home

Resting on a stone
by the bank of a beck
I wait for a heron, for such luck
as the bird can bestow.
The shadow of who I am
sits quietly beside me.
Seed-heads of swaying grasses
scatter insects like wishes.
Earth hums a plainsong of bees.

A clerical silhouette,
neck bowed as if in prayer,
is etched silent and still
amid the river's turbulence.
Meditation of feather and muscle
spears a silvery fish, rears
unfolding wings like a map
and gliding air streams,
carries me home.

Migration

She doesn't know the word for goose
me in a hoodie, her in a hijab
beside a canal clad in winter.

Big duck
she says, smiling
accepting the crust I offer.

Her hands cold
quietly mobile
like fish in shimmering water.

Casting crumbs
across the towpath
we laugh at the frenetic feeding.

Birds honking,
hissing, cackling
a crescendo, of noise, of survival.

Goose, I say
my finger points.
Geese, my arm arches a bridge.

Yes, in my homeland, geese
I saw, before the war.
Just luck she says, frowning

where the bread falls
where the bomb falls
who the shrapnel shatters.

She didn't know the word for goose
but she knew how to pluck pleasure
and meaning from a moment.

Arid

A Mediterranean sea sky.
Hebden Bridge basks
sunken valley dry
fear of floods forgotten.
Soil is chapped dust
wetland lips cracked
wildflowers wilting.
Tree roots suck hard
on straw hopes of rain.
Geese herd goslings
beside a draining canal.
A child's hopscotch
chalked on a street
isn't washed away.
Barbie and Ken dolls
sunbathe in beachwear
limbs at awkward angles
on a stone doorstep.
Flotsam balls of seed
dandelion tumbleweed
summersault pavements.
People in summer shorts
drink long bottled beers.
Only the beating of drums
suggests a world at war.

Groundcover

We kick them
into the long grass
those secrets
fearful of discovery
hiding amongst
whiskers of wild oats
ears of feral barley
brushes of fox sedge
those secrets
are nocturnal
with the musky stealth
of a reynard
hunter's eyes reflecting
the bones beneath
a pale moon's face.

Hebden Bridge

500 years of creativity and rain
siling down centuries
warping hills and rinsing rivers.

Seeping ancestors from wet soil
absorbed by trees
pulsing, rooting in peat.

Humans cautiously inhabit
this sunken land
formed by flood and artistry.

Woven from grief and grit
corded by veins
dripping DNA and industry.

Spores moulding the brain
but always a damp deliverance
ideas water born again.

Release

Our valley broods
holds its breath
pectin air thickens
sets as autumn jam
a mouthless whisper
quickening sap
anticipating storm
silence
stasis
still life
tapestry stretched taut
before the throat of thunder growls
and the forked tongues' lash
splatters bulging raindrops
like liquid eyes

Wading

A river broils anger
berates its bridges
drowns the siren
retches along streets
spits sticks and stones
breaks buildings and hearts

Pools in sodden rooms
stinking of sewerage
spoilt possessions piled high
words are washed empty
and ideas are debris
rinsed in anguish

After the flood
plastic trails in streamers
caught by floating tendrils
of torrent felled trees

Heavy machinery moves in
pumping burdened drains
sucking arteries and veins
flashing pools in neon light

A cat watches owl-eyed
wary from an upstairs window
cobbles seep silt and stream
riverbed stepping stones
and we take deep-dive breaths
knowing certainty is shallow

Pheasants roost at dusk
and water birds return
a dry forget-me-not sky
and a Russian poet reading
as a beck sings reconciliation
in a town translucent with shock

Across the Tops –
Hebden Bridge to Oxenhope

On the highest regular bus route in England
moors are mottled brown like an ancient hand
undulating relics of glacial erosion
a clenched fist.
We settle into bright seats under artificial light
cushioned with companions from the cold.
Our journey pierces another world
contoured across millennia
peat bog and blackened heather
warped by the grinding of time's gravity.

Shrieking wind damped by clammy mist
the vehicle's automated voice booms
but doesn't wink its headlights
as in a children's story book.
Accelerating, announcing the old names
of the lonely places where the ghosts gather
Crimsworth
Bedlam Road
Boundary Stone
scheduled stops just poles in the ground.

Christmas Passed

Words flap like washing in the wind
a palette of disappointment
drizzles from a shrouded sky.

A whisky bottle lies drunk
in a Methodist chapel graveyard
clinging to steep cobbles.

The river sloughs brown
in paths saturated with grief
running streams of gritted tears.

I rant against the rain
tasting despair deep in the gut
indigestible, iron-tinged.

Even the snow has forgotten
the shape of my solitary footprints.

Between the Stone

I exist
between the breathing of soil
the rasping of grit and stone
loose rocks beneath my feet
walking the turf roof
of my moorland world

Sculptured contours
hold water like cupped hands
an offering to the curlews
messengers of flight
cruising orchestral wind
across sky wells of light

I stagger
peat drunk into woodland
trees are gnarled beasts snarling
guarding undergrowth
stitched roots and leaf rot
dark matted memory

The ribcage of branches breaks
above a boulder anchored by hillside
within a ring of sunken earth

at its centre, a solitary stone seat
arbour armchair upholstered in moss
made by wizardry or weather

Origami buds folded nail hard on twigs
point like fingers on old mileposts
witness to natural magic
I sit
and resolve
to root myself here

Imbolc

This February a snow moon
glides white rays
feathering a blackberry sky.
Breath of a goddess
stirs the river, weaves water
in silver threads of hope
like swans slicing
the darkness.
A scent of quickening
as shoots thrust green
unfurling through soil.
Nothing is hidden
as light is given
in the awakening
of a new-born year.

The Seeding

Deep in the valley cleft
a willowy land-strip binds
hills shelved high
towering into library sky.

Flood plain tamed by men
dripping salt and sweat
gashing earth, hewing a canal
fortified by disembowelled stone.

Iron striking splintering rock
water harnessed to machinery
silenced the redshanks' cry
withered wetland plants
stunted Spring. Lost wildflowers
a beauty living now only in name
Mountain Everlasting, Moonwort,
Toothwort, Twayblade, Bur-marigold.

But moisture still veils the air
laces the hair of wild grasses
furs the trees with moss pelts
tangles reeds in damp welts.

Nature is reclaiming the soil
I've seen Pheasant's Eye bloom
heard Lilly-of-the Valley chime
sweet scent in woodland.

Summer Haze

I tell you you're a figment
of my imagination.
You don't believe me.

Sheep graze the sky
drifting wool, white
daubed with blue.
Fallowing the field below
where colour hums
yellow and purple.
Tasselled grasses wave
seas of grey-green
fine art brushes.

I touch silk
on shining buttercups
count clover trefoils
scatter petal confetti
pet dandelion pompoms
caress furred kitten
seed head tails
stroke ears of wild grain
like a lover.

Until only I remain.

Circling Forwards

I find you at dusk
I lose you at dawn
You are the night weaver
spinning my dreams
twisting the warp
securing the weft
lacing me tightly
into the straitening circle.

Torrential rain hisses
uncoiling pools
weather walking behind me
like an old dog
Woodpecker's percussion
drills into trees
Rune sticks
foretelling whittled sagas.

A theatre of crows
agitate a willow
My eyes scan branches
like a running squirrel
winged shadows squawk
I sense her before I see her
Druantia, bride of the oak

goddess of green magic.

Her voice is Imbolc
From damage and decay
new life is nurtured.

I find a truth
"My lover has left me
the thief of a night
stealing my joy."

Her fingers flutter
Love bares the root
The silver birch
Lady of the Woods
will cast her light
protect you from flood
gift you a healing.

A Midas sun
touches the valley gold
ferns dance playing tunes
on spiral fiddleheads.

Curled in their scrolls
are many stories of survival
amongst them mine
and maybe yours.

Bilberries

Before rain
on a sunken corpse way
glistening wet light
branches swimming air
tangles a bramble snare
scented by summer rot

I pick bilberries
tiny cogwheels
circling a season's time
black dots
like full stops
in green spiky script

I hold in my hand
purple beads
polished moorland pearls
indigo blots
raven black
midnight blue

I thread a necklace
spanning space between us
sending you a whisper

of wimberry
of windberry
of whortleberry

Conkers

I collect you
peeling leaves off polished teak.
You emerge sticky
from your spiked armour
shedding your green jerkins.
A medieval army, conquerors
marching through childhood.
The hard-nuts of nature.

Precious currency of playgrounds
wrinkled faces in chestnut hoods
you smell of soil and classrooms
under your glamorous silky sheen.
Holed and stringed you dangle
the jerking of marionettes
cracking sounds of cricket bats
wood on leather balls.

At home in adulthood
arranged on a white saucer
you look like a selection of pralines
smothered in rich dark chocolate.

November Dawning

You left me
                              alone
by the hither-stay stone
the frost moon medallion
silvering love's gloom.
Mist coils a beginning
seeping from peat soils.
Beneath the witness of trees
a breeze whispers my name.
As the sky thaws a dawn
from the light of darkness
I am reborn

The Calling

I hear
the songs of geese
as they fly in formation
Notes of feathers and freedom
cloud chords ascending, soaring grace
Beaks stretching, wing rhythms beating time
migrating landmass and limitless seas
Lakes glistening aquatic weed
silver scales reflecting
light in the glint
of eyes

Remembrance

After heavy Autumn rain
steaming as if from stewed tea
in translucent afternoon light
the ghosts of wet Sundays
seep up from cobblestones
smelling of blown heather.

Perhaps you still exist
in raindrops clinging to the bone
stalks of a season's debris.

I lie in crisping ferns
and see you in petal clusters
purple towers braiding sky
I am a child again
and you a young woman
our summers stacked before us.

Storm Shadow

Winter's cold talons claw
the backbone of England
Veined leaf skeletons rot
bones of summer flowering
Mist crochets a doily
woven across moorland
People ghost into greyness
time is moisture vaporising
Sun glimmers
a pewter tankard
unwilling to spill its liquid light
Trees droop sleet feathers
on a frozen fleece of garden wall
In the silence of snow I hear you
and ice tongues of fire speak

Church in Advent

'Nutcracker, it's a love story,' you say
and the ring on my finger winks
glints sun gold
shines moon silver.

The sugar plum fairy pouts
as the merry-go-round circles
unravelling tinsel music
from atop a biscuit tin.
Mother Ginger tastes the season
of Captain Candy sweetness.
Clara pirouettes in ballet grace
inventing a handsome prince.
And the rodent Mouse King rules.

Santa advertises coca-cola
in bright lurid flashing lights.
Baubles dangle like witch balls
from an artificial Christmas tree
centre stage before the altar.
A miracle of bananas
fruit of plastic evergreens
heaped on a foodshare table.
And old gods weep in woodland.

Up a spiral of steps, in an eaves room
a nativity set sighs, swaddling dust
from an old stone chimney
where trust and faith warm the hearth.

Hinterland

New Year is a performance
never to be previewed.
Time is yet to hang a costume
on the shape of who I'll be.

A hill above a valley pit.
Trees a dark melodrama.
Stars like stage lights
pinprick a backdrop sky.

Square eyes twinkle,
windows onto winter's dusk.
Floodlights tiering balconies
of stone spectators.

Actor and audience
we guess at an unwritten script.
Our end nothing more
than the wish of a curtain call.

Unbroken Line

Inside a mean council maisonette
you drew the most beautiful birds
Art was your adrenalin, along with sport
your thick fist weaving soft shapes
in fragile charcoal lines, skilfully drawn.
Big Daddy and racehorse commentary
the constant soundtrack of a Saturday.
After reading 'Iron Ladies
Why Women Vote Tory' I cried.
You died in 1979, struggling on sticks
To keep the blond bitch out.
"Don't you know that's sexist?" I'd shout
coming from you it made me sad.
Your heart broken
years before they said Britain had.
Funeral cakes and stand pies
men gazing into warm beer.
He was a champion, your Grandad. Boxer.
The pages of your sketchbooks forgotten
their tattered wings fading like memories.

Sunset

A brazier sun flames
forging desire.
Dragons fly west
breathing fire.
Sky is tidal estuary
an archipelago
of cloud.
Iridescent harbour light
guiding ships
at risk of passing in the night.

The Script

This love can only live
between the lines
of our raw poetry
Kisses only punctuate
the prose of fairy tales

But still I want
to meet you
in the blank pages
of our story

Beck Steed / Ceffyl Dwr

The water horse rears
a head of white spray
wet flanks glistening
Unbridled
a river runs through us
from source to sea
we ride the ebb and flow
an enchanted mount
Confluence
ocean eyes swimming
salt licked, wave lapped
Estuary.

Howling

We circle each other
wolves tethered
to a full moon
lolling tongues
which cannot stiffen
to shape the words
we fear to speak.

You make coffee
whisking almond milk
peaked froth evaporates
pitted by chocolate
and we take tepid sips
the moment waning
wet on our lips.

You Walk Beside Me

Beneath woodland architecture
where tree roots entwine
sap pulses veins
and dewy bluebells
ring joy
you walk beside me.

On a valley's heathery wingtips
where moor meets imagination
peat hallmarks centuries
and gravel-throated winds
whistle spring
you walk beside me.

Along the river artery
where amber beads of water
cut millstone grit diamonds
and daffodils bow
greeting sunlight
you walk beside me.

Under a hare moon
where liquid silver flows
sea waves of night

and owls call
enchanting flight
you walk beside me.

The Parting

We cross a bridge
lit by moon alchemy
over a dandelion and burdock beck
Guinness bitter in liquorice night.
A flower-faced owl soars
above a silent longing.
I am stretched on canvas
You are sketched charcoal
a shadow swallowed
by deep valley jaws.

Exposure

In this valley
hollowed by ice
between a canal
stagnating seasons
and a river
hurrying to the sea
beneath chimneys
outreaching spires
into delusional skies
I conjure
from the embers
of our Autumn
a winter sanctuary.
But there is no shelter
from your absence.

Another Place

Iron men, mesmerising power
stand staring seaward
faces hard, torsos barnacled
feet steadfast on shifting shores.

Statues ghosting landscape
turning dock cranes into toys
painted the primary colours
of childhood and certainty.

In heat haze they sway
as we dance mortal
to the ebb and flow of love
waltzing currents.

Salt stings our eager lips
preserving an inlet
where waves pan
grains of our existence.

Comfort

Older faces reflect opalescent
on the gleaming contours
of a Tiffany glass collection.

Two headed, we peer child-eyed
as brush strokes of sunlight paint
display cases in vivid palettes.

Skin mirrors the exhibits'
crazed spider web mosaics
the glazing of our outer selves.

We haven't faded
our colours are rich and deep
the vibrant oils of paradise birds.

Our friendship lime-green fresh
like the fern coiling delicate tendrils
around a sea-jade vase.

Years crinkle when we laugh
tinkling wrinkles of crystal joy
into echoing gallery air.

North Sea

Where hours are measured by tide
the Great Gull cries
brining seas with tears
Moon-breath waves
roll over rock pools
lit silver and jet

Stories are scrolls
stored in the shells
of creatures bidden
by trident gods
to tell in fossil and flotsam
stormy sagas
of oceans and shorelines

But only stone speaks
from cliffs gutted like fish
a language of rock
pitted poetry
hard consonants

Phantom Thought

You manifest from mist
like the stag men of old
but a round metal helmet
adorns your head, not antlers.
Monochrome sketch lines
shaping, solidifying
in the viscous moisture
of breath and moorland.
Wet flanks shining
leather and hide you ride
mane flowing, bag flapping
steel carbine glinting iron.
The last flickers of your light
heralds dusk, sparks legends.

Part Two - Poems in Prose

Tapestry

Hidden at the foot of a cloven valley, where mist hems the hills and the upper branches of trees, is a shop. It sells 'fine textiles crafted for discerning clientele,' or so the sign creaking outside claims.

Gaia hesitates on the worn stone threshold. She grasps her purse and her coat pocket bulges like a reptile feeding. She pushes at a reluctant heavy door.

A woman, head bowed and back curved, weaves on a wooden loom in the dim interior. Her hands are small and supple, her fingers swimming with darting silvery skill between the threads.

She conjures waves of colour stretching warp to weft. As she works she sings. The songs of migrating birds, the shanties of sea creatures calling. Her tapestry grows, ridged with texture. The colours deepen. Rich vibrant hues hum as the beam breathes, falls and rises.

The woman has a special commission, a project of such importance that she cannot pause to acknowledge Gaia's presence. Small pools of water shine like fish scales at her feet as she weaves rivers and darns glaciers. Smiling, she stitches trade routes across continents and braids cultures.

A wispy man with thin lips appears from the back of the shop and greets Gaia. He searches racks of wooden shelves, stroking his white beard and repeating the words, "beautiful bedspreads," like a mantra. He selects several coverlets reverently. The shades and patterns of Earth pile up on the glass counter. Gaia chooses a patchwork in a palette of blue, turquoise and jade.

Card payments are regrettably not possible, a notice in bold black letters informs customers. The man nods curtly as Gaia unrolls crisp ten-pound notes which smell of expectation and hands them to him. She leaves the shop hugging the world, wrapped neatly in brown paper.

That night, Gaia smooths the new counterpane across her bed, admiring its harmony of art and nature. She sleeps deeply and dreams of pristine white ice sheets starched in moonlight.

The Game

Linda has spied a brown house moth beating its filigree wings against the inner glass pane of a cabinet. Something beginning with "f," she says to herself, opening the door with a small key. The moth flutters into the room.

"Life's just like a series of children's party games - don't you think, Mark?" Linda's green eyes are looking at the floor, to the right of her slippers. A thought then, not an emotion observes Mark with relief. He's learnt a lot from the co-counselling course Linda insisted he attend.

"Is it?" he responds, focussing on the pink pompoms twitching at the end of Linda's feet. He definitely doesn't agree that life is like a series of children's games, but he doesn't want to risk contradicting her. As his Mum once said (prior to the marriage), Linda could be "temperamental."

"Yes, take Pass the Parcel for instance, more false endings than any film or symphony. The music stops, you have your chubby, sticky fingers on the colourful wrapping paper…"

"Newspaper." Mark's mother had always wrapped the parcel in newsprint, decorative paper was too good for children to tear and shred. "What a waste, it will never do," was a constant refrain as he was growing up.

"...but after ripping off one layer, often hurting your hands in the process, there's no present, no prize, just another layer of wrapping and the eternally jangling, irritating tune plays mockingly on. Then you have to give the package to the next child who might win and you don't even like them, they smell or call you names in the playground."

"Mmm," Mark isn't listening, he's learnt the skill of making what he hopes are appropriate noises which release him from any obligation to converse with his wife.

"I had a best friend Jenny whose Mum was a bit bohemian and put a sweet in each layer, but it wasn't always a consolation. Sometimes the toffee jumped out of the paper, hurtling across the room into someone else's grasp, where it was immediately shoved into the mouth so they wouldn't have to give it back. Finders, keepers.

And then there's Musical Chairs! That's another game we're forced to play throughout our lives. All that jostling, pushing, pulling, running, desperation to get your own bottom on the ever-diminishing number of chairs. Survival of the fittest. You're lucky if you come away with just bruises. It was always the biggest, heaviest boy who won. Brute force beat any positioning strategy. When the music stops you're stranded, marooned on an island of carpet, entirely alone, sidelined and defeated while those who still have a seat in the game grin triumphantly." Linda sits down heavily in her favourite armchair, breathless after her monologue.

Mark watches a strand of late afternoon sunlight lengthen across the sofa. The plush blue fabric faded a little more each year and its high back blocked the view across the wooded valley from the bay window, but Linda insisted all the furniture should face inwards. One of her friends was an advocate of Feng Shui and Linda had the passion of a convert, talking enthusiastically about the need for Qi energy flow to create wellbeing. Also she considered it more sociable, not that they ever had any visitors. His wife was always out, having coffee with her crones after an art or yoga class. Mark meets up with his mates in the pub where their conversation is about football or indie bands. Logically he can't imagine their separate social circles overlapping as the Venn diagrams he'd drawn at school had done. His phone vibrates but he resists the urge to pick it up. He doesn't want to deal with Linda's inevitable curiosity about who was texting him, or what they'd said.

"I'm still not comfortable in this living room," Linda scowls. "The five elements aren't balanced."

"Four elements," Mark retorts, "there are four elements; fire, water, earth and air."

"No five; fire, water, earth, wood and metal."

"I've never heard anyone say their star sign is wood or metal."

"Whatever." Linda turns toward the light where the moth has flattened itself against a net curtain. Its antennae are trembling weakly, a scaley powder smeared around its silhouette.

"You're losing all your magic dust," thinks Linda.

"We should get rid of it," says Mark in an effort to escape the stalemate, "this old carpet. I could sand the floorboards. More wood."

"Are you sure you're up to that? It's hard work. All the furniture would need to be moved from the room. And messy, huge dunes of sawdust to clear. Then there's the varnishing, which means toxic fumes. But you're right, perhaps I should look for some more wooden ornaments."

"That's just what we need, another marquetry box for you to display your trinkets in. A perfect match for all the thick-set, dark wood furniture you've bought "cheaply" from charity shops."

"Simon Says, do this, do that. Don't do this, don't do that. Only in this house it's Mark Says. Well I'm tired of your games. Would we even recognise each other if we played Blind Man's Bluff nowadays? Spun round, feeling the contours of each other's face, dizzy and sick."

"Buff," says Mark, "not Bluff. Buff! It's the old English word for shove."

Linda stands abruptly. "I'm through playing Hide and Seek. I've been so busy trying to find you all these years, I haven't been able to see myself. Well I'm taking my blindfold off, right now, so I can Pin the Tail on the Donkey with absolute precision."

"Hee, haw," Mark brays, but the front door has already slammed shut.

Journey of the Light

I

At the crossroads, where the yew tree guards the boundary between this world and the next and the devil lurks, the hermit joins us. He is not a bearer of coffins but a carrier of weighty secrets, slipping silently into step at the rear of our cortege. His cornflower eyes gaze into an overcast sky, searching for angels, cloud wings under which to shelter or hide. As we walk, our feet seem to follow the swaying rhythm of the witch balls hung along the road. The common belief is that the threads and charms inside them will catch and tangle any passing evil spirits.

Our knees bent to the creaking of the wooden casket, we ascend a steep track that winds through the wood. A pilgrimage of trees marks the path. The oak king, ruler of the warmer months, marshals the ash, the elder, the beech and the silver birch, but even he cannot control the goat willow, its cats' tails powder the coarse grass yellow. I pick a rowan twig and put it into my pocket, to protect my father from lingering in this earthly world, to banish all thought of the cloven-hoofed one.

"A good man, your father. You needn't worry about his crossing," John smiles at me and I wonder how he crunches so many funeral biscuits with so few teeth wobbling in his pale gums. A regular walker of the corpse ways, enjoying the ale and the company, John is always welcome because he brings with him kind words and a fine voice to lead the singing.

Bluebells haze purple, toll the passing of our seasons. At our feet, stones glow in the Spring sunlight, illuminated manuscripts of insects and birds. A single white foxglove blooms foetal promises of summer.

Soon the procession will be complete. After the Lily Hall cottages there will be no more followers to collect before the arduous climb to our mother church. The four stout men carrying the coffin are bowed beneath its weight, their breath labouring like penitents.

I can see the hither-stay stone now, a flat shelf sticking out from the mossy hill beside the path. Only a few more yards and we can rest awhile. I adjust the leather strap of the bag that hangs awkwardly from my shoulder. I am proud of the arval biscuits packed inside. I baked them yesterday, carving a cross into the centre of each one and decorating the edges with a fork while the dough was still soft. I used all the honey we had in the house to make them. It isn't wise to scrimp and save with funerals, you risk offending the living, or the dead.

My father is lowered in a silence that speaks of straining sinews and parched throats. Mother anxiously checks that the bearers have laid the coffin correctly, with father's feet facing the direction in which we are to travel. There are many cautionary tales of corpses carried headfirst to the cemetery finding their way back to earthly homes as spirits. It is barely a year since our neighbours lost a child to the sweating sickness. Folks said too much ale had been consumed by the mourners and the small corpse was carried to the church headfirst, the mistake only being discovered at the graveside. There were rumours too that the funeral procession had strayed from the corpse way. Farmer Greenwood swears that those of his fields which flank the path have been barren ever since. On cold winter nights his family have heard the spirit crying, a disembodied wailing at their back door.

Mother and my sisters line up to the right of the coffin. The other mourners are bunched on the left of it. I offer the biscuits to eager hands. The hermit folds his hands together as if to pray and bows his head in humility. He is the last to stretch out his fingers, they brush warm across my palm. After we have eaten the sins of the deceased, Mother passes round the large jug of ale which glints amber like the peat beck we have yet to cross on our journey. I know traversing the clapper bridge is a practical necessity, it's also a wise precaution. Carrying the departed over running water ensures they cannot return home to haunt the living. It is awkward manoeuvring the coffin onto the long stone slab that balances on a pier of boulders, but not as arduous as the washing, winding and watching rituals we have performed to prepare our father's body for burial. After the scrubbing of our cottage threshold, and the lugging of wooden furniture into different positions to confuse and deter any returning spirit, Mother's hands were chapped, and as red as her tearless eyes.

We chant our prayers, voices rising like swirling curlews. John starts the hymns, his tenor rolling across the hillside. We sing for my father's salvation.

Our column snakes onwards. The moor is scarred by the narrow stone path like a fossil of the landscape, as we, the living, begin to walk again. For those of us striding beside the coffin the springy new growth of heather and gorse lightens our steps, if not our hearts. At the whispering corner on the edge of the hilltop village, where the low stone dwellings cling precariously to the craggy outcrop, we halt. We listen. Is that the coarse grass moving in the breeze, or the low indistinct voices of the dead murmuring? The pall bearers quicken their steps, eager to reach the sanctuary of the lynch gate, to shelter beneath its roof; to hand over the burden of the soul, which unlike the body doesn't always lie still. Their clogs strike, iron on cobble, along the path which leads them deosil toward the church as the bell begins its toll.

The minister waits, hands clasped over his cassock, his gown floating like the pinion feathers of a jackdaw. His face is expressionless beneath his black cap. He signs a cross in the air, a signature of his office, before greeting us with arms outstretched. We have fulfilled our duty by bringing the dead for burial in consecrated ground at the mother church. It is his responsibility to ensure custom is followed according to canon law to secure the salvation of another soul. The priest ignores the hermit handing out small branches of yew gathered from the churchyard to family mourners, but his puffy face reddens with irritation. He is tolerant of the old beliefs, his church has incorporated many of the ancient rites into Christian theology, and the congregation are on the whole godly people. But hermits? He will have no truck with hermits, particularly those who seek to undermine the authority invested in him by holy order and apostolic succession.

The yew branch is sticky. Its needles pricking at my hands like a pecking hen. A red admiral butterfly flutters momentarily above my father's coffin. The hermit's eyes look directly into mine, and the firmament of the sky seems to be transposed.

"The promise of resurrection is sealed with its angel kiss," he whispers. I feel the warmth of his breath on my cheek, then, like the butterfly, it has flown.

The procession swells into the church which reeks of tallow, damp prayer books and the faithful. The psalms and hymns are hazy and I find them no comfort. I try not to shuffle on the hard pew. The priest's voice drifts, I hear his words of hope, but they are buffeted in my head, as if he is speaking from a windy hill crest; "At the general resurrection on the last day, we may be found acceptable in thy sight."

I love my God, but I do not want to meet him yet or join my father on this journey.

We bear the coffin to the churchyard where a rich scent of newly-dug soil hovers over a deep gash in the earth, fortified by wooden stakes at its crumbling corners. I see small shoots of green beside the grave, shy pledges of new life.

"We now commit our brother's body to the ground; earth to earth, ashes to ashes, dust to dust; in sure and certain hope of the resurrection to eternal life." Last night Mother saw corpse candles, wispy blue flames flitting low over stony ground, traveling the route from our cottage to the cemetery.

Tonight I will gaze into the sky to watch my father's spirit illuminated by angels in a kingdom of clouds. I may be blessed by a single soft feather from their wings floating down into my world.

II

I stand under a cloudy sky on a night as empty of stars as it has so far been of sleep. The tiny flames which drew my curiosity out into the enveloping dark are still flickering. Each flame is as blue as the pilot light on a gas boiler. They move low to the ground, brushing the tops of grasses rustling in the breeze. I remember reading somewhere about will-o-the-wisps, wandering lost souls who lead travellers astray. Switching my torch on quickly the light is strong, obliterating the small flames like a fire extinguisher. As the beam searches my fear seems foolish. The call of an owl heightens the density of the darkness. I sense the fetid warmth of the hunter's presence, close, very close. I am unlikely to sleep now. It is almost dawn. Before leaving the house I'd thrown on a waterproof jacket and hiking boots, so I decide to walk. I follow the steep flagstone path of the old corpse way through Mytholm Wood to Heptonstall, hoping to see the spire of the winter saint's church baptised by the first rays of the sun.

A silk black night, the moon a pearl shelled in cloud. The way ahead is more overgrown than I remember, daytime familiarity submerged in caverns of gloom. Branches lurch at me and I have to swerve to avoid their grasping twig fingers. The barbs of tall brambles tangle in my hair and I remove them with cold, trembling hands. I feel a slow trickle of blood flowing from my forehead and congealing in my left eyebrow.

Where the path widens I sit on a flat-topped boulder projecting from the steep mossy bank. The path ahead is shrouded by a regiment of trees in palisade rows. One fallen elder lies with open mouth, bearded by broken roots. In the far distance there is a glow of red-eyed coals heaped on the ground. I rise and stumble onwards- onwards towards the smouldering embers and their promise of warmth.

There is a circular glade on a grassy knoll. The trees guarding the clearing are gnarled in wisdom, branches reaching for the sky dome above. At first I think I see a group of small nocturnal mammals standing in the moonlight, but they remain still on my approach and reveal themselves to be rocks, furred with moss. The distant ringing of bells turns out to be a tiny stream channelling starlight. Just discernible on the circumference of the enclosure is a shelter constructed of timber. It leans into the trees for support, tethered by rope.

I sit by a small firepit, stones carefully placed to keep the flames at bay. A twig cracks like a starting pistol. Alarm blasts into my head as a small man with a bright yellow blanket wrapped around his shoulders emerges from the woodland. Fright subsides to a sensible wariness; his voice is as warm as his fire.

"Hello," he says, “may I accompany you to St. Thomas a Becket? I too am a holy traveller and there are many dangers on our route."

I want to say I'm not holy, but even unspoken this sounds rude, so I simply blurt out, "Yes." Then by way of explanation. "The clapper bridge is narrow and slippery, risky on your own."

He folds his fingers together as if to pray and stares directly at me. Even In the firelight his eyes are cornflower blue. Holding out his hand, he beckons.

I nod in response, and we walk, him leading, me following, silence between us. My torch beam clings to the squelching ground, revealing matted leaf mould. There is a lightening of the night sky and of my footfall. Above us the arms of the world circle an embrace. Branches breathe more deeply as if awakening from a long slumber.

At the crossroads, beside the corrugated bark of the yew tree, the man kneels; "Evergreen, the old wizard of the wood has seen many Advents, many Lents and humbly wears the purple of repentance."

"Isn't the yew tree poisonous?" I can't resist responding. "The witches in Macbeth brew a deadly drink containing 'slips of yew silvered in the moon's eclipse'."

"The yew tree embraces death as part of life. Longbows are made from its timber. Yew branches are pliant, growing back into the earth to birth new seedlings, their reincarnation."

"Do you believe in reincarnation?" I ask.

"I don't believe in reincarnation; I live it and die it." His words soar strong yet soft, like wings.

Maybe it's the intimacy of the early dawn, the witness of trees, the scent of resin, which combine to make me feel safe, accepted, bold enough to confide; "Sometimes I sense a recognition, certain places, certain people. I feel I know you from a long time ago, we walked in woodland where wild forget-me-nots grow."

He doesn't comment but turns and looks at me, really sees me, and smiles a welcome.

"We have a choice here, laid out in stone before us." He points to the fork in the old packhorse trail, "the path of fear or the path of love."

I hesitate to select a route. Both of them appear to course upwards in the direction of the church. "Doesn't the devil lurk at crossroads," I say mischievously.

"The devil does not exist!" His voice chimes clear and strident, "Ony God is real. The devil is illusory, manifested from the shadows of human fear."

I suddenly know this to be true and wonder why something so simple and obvious has eluded me for many years, perhaps for many lives; "So the devil deceives us into thinking he exists."

He grins, "You can learn a lot from paradoxes; about yourself, other people, different worlds, why things happen and why they don't." Taking the right-hand track, he strides ahead.

We are rising with the sun and arrive breathless at the plateau on top of the headland just as the first radiance of a new day shimmers gold across the church spire of St. Thomas a Beckett.

It is Winter Solstice. In light of the darkness, I understand.

Brided

The women flutter in shades of pink, yellow, and periwinkle-blue like tiny butterflies. Wedding guests collecting nectar, sucking sweetness from the sugary occasion. The bride is alabaster, a statue glistening in sunshine. The men's suits are sober, unlike their slightly crumpled wearers. The bridegroom is in black, a mourning he doesn't yet comprehend. Oil painted in racing silks the females are corralled into an emerald field hedged with hawthorn and wild parsley.

From Carol's vantage point on the hill, next to the solidity of a nineteenth century stone tower, the figures are frail toys. There is a sickly pastoral smell; hay and dried dung.

Carol is uncomfortably hot, a ripening beetroot red. She was once a bride, slim and sure of herself. The years have padded her, physically and psychologically. She has learnt to control feelings which once were tidal. Now she just has to manage the flotsam and jetsam of life constantly being washed up on her beach.

Her husband is angry, Carol has forgotten the parcel of cheese 'n' pickle sandwiches she'd prepared and wrapped in clingfilm for their picnic. Instead, she has inadvertently packed half a loaf of dry bread into the basket of food and placed it carefully in the boot of his new car. Their car, Carol corrects herself. She had paid half the cost of the BMW but had never driven it; nervous in case she scratched the shiny metallic surface or put a dent into one of its perfect gleaming wings.

Her offer of a packet of crisps and a chocolate biscuit does not console him. Carol decides not to suggest having lunch in the pub. Her husband thinks eating out is a waste of money and anyway it is likely the bride and groom have booked the entire restaurant. He strides scowling towards the obelisk, binoculars bouncing against his paunch. His heavy footsteps are a thudding bass below the trill of chatter from the distant party.

Carol hopes the young couple will have a long and happy marriage, will be kind companions once their passion is spent. As inevitably it will be, just like foreign currency when you're on holiday. Carol still considers marriage to be a good institution, on the whole, all things considered. Certainly, she regards it as good for society, for stability, for maintaining a semblance of order. The wedding industry generates money for religious establishments, she muses, and more recently for listed buildings too. It keeps clerics out of trouble; sustains jobs in catering, fashion and chauffeuring, albeit with low wages. Even when marriages fail, at least family lawyers succeed.

She hadn't vowed to obey her husband, but she had taken his name, and in practice did defer to him in almost all aspects of her life. She had discovered early on in their marriage that she had little appetite for argument. It threatened to unearth her buried treasure chest of joy, which she kept to herself, locked and secure.

Carol saunters through long grass with seeded plumes. It sways gracefully, waltzing with the yellow lips of toadflax and the purple heart-shaped petals of dog violets. The air is warm and tranquil. She cannot see or hear her husband now.

The tight knot of wedding guests unravels as they wind up the hill in small groups towards the Pike. A murmur of voices rises above the rustling of the meadow. At first Carol can't distinguish words in the polite hum of conversation, but soon she hears a pronouncement that the monument will provide a romantic setting for the photographs.

The miniature people gradually grow as they approach her, the women's chiffon scarfs rippling like the pennants of an attacking army. The bride billows white, a lone flag of surrender. She is making slow progress up the incline, encumbered by high heels and her long dress. The bridesmaids' gait is awkward as they hold the lacy train above the dust, worrying about rips and stains.

Carol's pupils narrow as she focuses on an older woman in an elaborate hat sporting a peacock feather which wobbles in time with her flesh. A serviette in the woman's hand waves as she dabs her face. Wiping sweat or tears? Happiness or sorrow? Carol isn't sure.

She watches the photographer gesticulating wildly as he arranges the company for the obligatory group picture. The motor of his camera sounds like distant machine gun fire as he takes multiple shots in rapid succession.

The kiss Carol's husband lands on her forehead is unexpected. His face is so close it blurs. His smile is conciliatory.

"If we leave now, we'll catch the café open at the ice cream farm," he says.

Carol lowers her head and twists her wedding ring. Guilt flames her cheeks. Not because she had forgotten the sandwiches, but because she has a secret lover with eyes as blue as summer skies.

Stage the Masque

I stand on an arched eyebrow of a familiar terraced street at the edge of town. Wheelie bins stagger at drunken angles on the steep slope. Stone houses crouch on the last strip of pavement before a hinterland scrub, claimed neither by humanity nor nature. Damp early morning air curls like wood smoke, veiling the lives of those who live here. The street is deserted, apart from two women hunched against the cold like perching ravens. I can see them look towards Fae's house and I can guess what they are saying. They're gossiping about her disappearance.

"I had my suspicions," one of the women purses her lips, sucking through the giddy straw of disapproval, "but I didn't want to be a nosey neighbour."

"She wasn't one for socialising. I was never invited in. She'd leave you stood on the back doorstep."

"And him a happily married man."

"With two dogs."

As I draw closer, quietly and slowly so they don't notice me, their voices drop to a whisper.

"In the cellar they found meat hooks and baby dragons."

"Marionettes," I correct them, but only in my mind. I definitely don't want to catch their attention. Fae is an artist, into fantasy and folklore, walking in other worlds kind of stuff. Worlds they couldn't see.

The women snort, steaming like mules in the cold air.

"They carried on like a couple of teenagers in love for the first time. And both their heads grey."

"Any road, she's flitted now, owing rent too I bet." They stamp their feet before turning abruptly to go into their respective homes. As I leave their conversation behind me and climb the stone flags that ascend the hillside into woodland, I carry Fae's indignation with me like a dark shadow.

Fae drank, not alcohol as was often alleged, but ginger and lemon tea. I'd sip the sharp, amber liquid without comment. Not with expectation of enjoyment but because I craved her company and creativity. She painted colour, in bold abstract oils, into my life. She swirled excitement and daubed hope in intricate patterns that mapped life's convolutions. 'Love without Fear' was her motto. She embodied it, whether eating thick slices of vegan chocolate cake, or when she was poised like Athena in front of a large blank canvas, absorbed in her art.

I am worried about Fae and wonder if she'll reappear. She is my soulmate.

I didn't know she'd planned to go, but I do know her rent is paid. The women are also wrong about the lovers being old. It is their story that is old, has seen saplings mature into ancient trees hallowed by age and inhabited by faeries.

My listening tree awaits, patient and wise. The large burr on its wrinkled bark always reminds me of an elephant's ear, dark-grey and mottled. The woods are my other world. Rocks sleep like hoary beasts within the hillside. I hear the sound of running water translate into the Wild Hunt, searching for the sea, the source, in a clamour of horns. Underfoot the leaf mould is khaki-brown. A magpie calls out to me from the mist of the morning twilight, neither moon nor sun is visible. I stride along the mossy path, veer into a thicket, and reaching the clearing sit comfortably at the base of my tree, which never forgets our previous conversations.

"I've often told you love would nourish me, set me free," I confess, "but it's imprisoned me, and I pace around its compound. I've trodden the earth down flat so that nothing living can grow." A rustle of sympathy flutters through the crisp, dry leaves sprinkled around the slab of a nearby boulder.

"I'll tell you my story from the start." I'm always more eager to share beginnings, they can be as pure and clear as a raindrop. Endings usually torrent in beads of hail that sting.

"We met on the moors. He was walking two cocker spaniels marked like dominoes.

I patted the dogs and their tails waved in the coarse long grass which swayed like a great inland sea around the roughly hewn pillar, known as Churn Milk Joan. I asked him what the dogs were called, too shy to ask him directly the questions I really wanted answered.

"Oberon and Puck," he smiled; "I wanted to call them Bottom and Puck, but my wife was horrified, said she'd be embarrassed shouting for Bottom in the park."

Had I slipped into a mid-afternoon's dream? I was light-headed, giddy as a dragonfly, and lent against the stone for support. White light was spreading across the ground like spilt milk.

"What do you think happened to Churn Milk Joan?" He definitely had my scent. "Was it foxes, a man, or just bitter cold that clawed and killed her? Did she freeze to death in a blizzard on this very spot?" If he intended to impress me by referring to the Ted Hughes' poem, it was working.

"I believe it's a cautionary legend to warn maids from straying from the path," I answered, "morally perhaps more than literally."

He placed his foot into the indent around the base of the standing stone. "We stand at an ancient intersection, a meeting of three parish boundaries. This is the omphalos of the breathing moor."

I ran my fingers round the hollow cup on the top of Churn Milk Joan, sending the coins in it spinning; "A gift to the spirit world to bring good luck, or a tradition originating from it being a plague stone." I rummaged in my pockets but they were empty.

"Here," his warm fingers and a cold wedding ring brushed my palm as he placed a pound in my hand. I felt a momentary quiver before dropping it into the hollow, where it shocked the pooled rain-water into concentric circles.

His voice was wistful: "I've hiked up here on New Year's Eve several times, avoiding Hogmanay parties, but I've never seen the stone spin round three times when the midnight bells at St. Michael's Church ring in the valley below."

"My friend calls it Churn Milk Peg," I said, "named for the old woman who is guardian of nut thickets. She is a wood spirit who protects soft un-ripe fruit from human foragers. Sometimes you can see the smoke from her pipe rising above the moor."

He laughed; 'There are few trees up here and certainly no nut bearing ones, but I have seen wisps of fog curling out of the peat bog. Smoke signals from other worlds. This stone marks a boundary, not just geographically." He held out his hand. I grasped it with an eagerness which surprised me.

"Colin," he said.

"Alice," I responded.

Our handclasp endured until he asked, "Would you like a coffee?"

He released my fingers, shrugged off his backpack and pulled out a small flask. The coffee was strong and sweet.

"I'll be at the Bridestones this time next week." Colin stood up and departed quickly, the dogs trotting at his heels. He didn't turn around and I watched him shrinking with each stride, until he merged with the grainy horizon."

Branches stir and creak gently before settling again in silent repose. The tree and I have a relationship based on respect, so I don't reveal everything. I wouldn't want to scare it or try the patience of many seasons. I never mention Fae because she would disrupt our dialogue, make it difficult to understand. I didn't tell it that after my first meeting with Colin I walked home with Spring in my steps and in my heart. Or that as soon as I had a signal on my phone, I searched for the meaning of the word "omphalos." The medical term for navel or more generally the centre of something, a hub. I saw radiating spokes, shiny rays of possibility, a bicycle wheel revolving, ravelling out distance and time.

It has been six long days since the arrangement with Colin. The next day sees a dragon's breath wind chasing fiery clouds across a duck-egg sky, dawn's red warning. I hurriedly dress in the protection of full waterproofs, jacket and trousers. My boot laces knot awkwardly. I make a flask of ginger and lemon tea and pack two bags of salted cashew nuts. I am still thinking of Churn Milk Peg, although legends associated with the Bridestones are very different. I know this because I have done my research in anticipation of another talk from Colin.

The shrieking of the wind intensifies as I ascend to Bridestones Moor. The rough grass tangles like long hair on a pelt. I'm unsteady on the spongy ground. It is ribbed with undulations of rock. I spot him immediately, a flash of orange among the boulders. He is sitting beneath the Bride Stone itself, leaning against its whittled base eroded by wind and water. I fear the towering mass of the outcrop may topple so I lower myself carefully beside him.

"I was expecting you. I've left Oberon and Puck at home; dogs ruin a good picnic." Colin stretches an arm out to tap a wicker basket. The tea and cashew nuts suddenly seem inadequate contributions to his lunch plans. "It's a strenuous hour's walk but that's less than the effort of a moment compared to the millennia that have formed these rocks, created the Anvil and the Sphinx."

"Don't forget the Obscene Cleft." He obviously doesn't find my comment amusing. I am conscious of trying to catch my breath and of the sweat trickling down my back as I add quickly, "The romance of many wedding ceremonies still echoes within that Bridestone."

"The Bride Stone itself is probably named after Brigid, the goddess of Imbolc, who heralds the coming of spring," he says this while beginning to unpack the picnic. Five wedges of cheese, all individually wrapped in wax paper, blue-veined, smoked, soft and hard, creamy and nutty, are placed next to cherry tomatoes strung like bunting on the vine. A slab of butter in a plastic container, a box of crackers in assorted shapes, seeded and plain, and a jar of onion relish completes the feast spread across a chequered cloth. There are two small plates and an array of knives, some curved and some pointed.

I'm embarrassed by the lavishness of his preparations and stare at the horizon which is forging a gathering black cloud. On the other side of the valley I can just discern the Old Woman crags looming out of a darkening sky.

"Cailleach, the Old Woman who sculpts outcrops with a hammer," I'm determined to use my newly acquired knowledge of folklore. "The veiled one, queen of winter, goddess of frost, ice, and bitter winds. She ensures the seasons' wheel turns smoothly."

"It's pronounced Karl-he-hach," he croons.

The first raindrops are sharp and hard, like crystal tears.

"It might just be a shower," but Colin has already begun to pack the wicker basket. His lips a clenched line scarring his face, his teeth a portcullis guarding his mouth.

I make a tentative suggestion, "We could walk back to my house and have an indoor picnic." Then I have a moment of uncertainty. "But that might be too far for you and also I reckon the chances of the crackers remaining dry are slim." I'm not sure I want him to know where I live.

His face stretches to a smile, "I can't think of anyone I'd rather eat soggy crackers with."

Afterwards, when I consult Fae about what happened, joking that our clothes were so wet we had to remove them, how I needn't have been concerned about the state of my lounge because the carpet became covered in crumbs, her eyes glitter with mischief and joy.

"Were you both greedy? What were his table manners like? A swan song of love." She continues, reading volumes into my silence. "Pure, white and feathered, soaring on the wings of angels. The swan is a bearer of spiritual medicine, navigating the river of life with grace, a guide to transformative journeys. Swans symbolise fidelity. They mate for life."

Occasionally Fae irritates me, "Well he clearly doesn't."

Fae doesn't like to be contradicted, "White is a colour of many shades. It has a universal quality. It floats effortlessly but weighs us down. It cannot be classified."

"Love is a four-letter word," I retort.

Guilt stalks me. It smells of dark chocolate. It appears as a grinning imp out of the grey patinas of dry stone walls when I am walking. At night I dream of riding dragons above fields mantled in wildflowers. The serpent squirms beneath me, rising and falling with my breath. Its hot mouth opens and fire lashes through woodland where bluebells sound a warning.

"If you could turn a bluebell flower inside out without tearing it you'd win the heart of the one you love." Fae's voice is incessant, even in sleep. I resolve not to contact Colin but I haven't thrown away the slip of paper he has written his number on. I have studied the numerals, tried but failed to find meaning in their random patterns.

"Hidden in the petals of flowers you will discover geometric forms relating to the mathematical laws which govern our planet," Fae advises. "You should search for cowslips; their blooms are the keys to open the door to Freyja's secret hall with its treasure of inner knowledge." I ignore her, but the voice echoes in the dream vaults of my head. "At least look for some St. John's wort to help you fight off your demons."

It's been raining all week which is one reason I've not been back to visit my tree. Instead I've been unpacking after the move. I flick at dust that circles in the air like small midges above a pond. Inevitably it settles again on the clutter of ornaments which I don't particularly like but dutifully hold on to, because they have some stale sentimental value. I make good progress sorting through clothes and watch with satisfaction as a bag destined for the charity shop swells and bulges like an overweight stomach. Fae has a different idea of style to me. She is fond of pixie boots, patterned leggings, and swirling blouses with long flowing sleeves. Her fashion sense is definitely influencing me, it is the dark, baggy items that I choose to ditch.

When I'm taking old, 'previously loved' clothes out to the recycling bin I notice the flowers. A bunch of red tulips, petals funnelled tight like bright turbans on slender necks, protected by a collar of leaves. The handwritten note is sodden, but the blotted words are still decipherable. "We could dance. There's a gig on at the Dog, Friday 8.30."

The tulips thrill Fae. "They symbolise love, renewal, and hope," she declares. "It is said that a humble stonecutter fell in love with a Persian princess and sought to win her hand in marriage. Her father, the king, horrified at the thought of such a match, challenged the suitor to carve a path through the mountain that separated them. Determined he tunnelled to reach his beloved. But when he succeeded the king broke his word and deceitfully told the young man that his daughter, Shirin, was dead. Raging with grief the stonecutter rode his horse off a cliff. When she learnt of her lover's death Shirin plunged over the same precipice. From the earth stained with their blood tulips sprang forth."

It sounded more like a story of despair than of hope to me, but Fae's enthusiasm is insidious. I decide to join Colin on Friday night.

The 'Dog and Goose' is a pub which crouches, pensive, on the towpath of a canal carved through a steep valley. Its stone exterior was once painted white, but is now a tobacco-yellow, stained like the fingers of the men who have smoked there over the centuries. The head of a dog growls on the sign which hangs above the entrance. It grates as it swings slowly in the wind. No fresh air penetrates the dark interior. Mullioned windows block the light. Low beams soak up the souls of those lost here. The round tables and bar stools are pushed back to the perimeter of one large room. They surround a circular space which looks like a fighting pit. A yeasty smell of old stories and new dreams greets me as I enter.

"Alice," Colin beckons me towards the bar, where he is deep in conversation with the bartender. "This is Mick. He's a promoter as well as keeping the pub. The band arrived on time so they've finished the soundcheck. I wanted to be early so you could have a seat. They're in short supply. It'll be packed in an hour. What are you drinking?"

"House white for me please." When it arrives the wine is warm and the fluted glass looks precarious beside Colin's pint.

"The Shadow Puppets, Indie band, Madchester era." Mick informs me. Colin stares into his beer. Then I stir my own recollections into his cloudy pool.

"I was there, Manchester I mean, in the '80s … the early '90s.. The Hacienda was my regular haunt, recreational drugs being passed round like sweets, and burly men in tutu dresses. Quivering angel wings attached to gyrating unisex bodies. The pulse of the music throbbed beneath our skin, synchronised with our heartbeat."

"I was there too, in the Hulme Crescents," Mick is apparently more interested than Colin in hearing about my Manchester youth. "Circus skills and cockroaches were my chief concerns back then." Mick grins; "No rent to worry about, we were all squatters and the council didn't care because the deck-access flats were due for demolition anyway."

"My best friend at the time lived in the Redbricks."

"Ah, the Redbricks, 1940s art deco, posh part of the council estate. Homes fit for heroes, although it was antiheroes living there in our time. Not that the Crescents didn't have a lot to offer. The water was free, and you could get electricity connected if you paid for it. There was a real Bohemian vibe. A creative city in the sky, with clowns, acrobats, artists, writers and musicians meeting on the concrete walkways." Mick is in danger of being drowned out of his reverie by the growing gaggle of people at the bar. "The Hacienda never made any money," he shouts, "hardly any alcohol was sold there. Folks on ecstasy asked for water rather than ale." On this note Mick's attention turns to those waiting at his own bar. Orders are placed and his arms draw several pints from different pumps simultaneously like an octopus.

The venue is filling up fast, mostly with blokes in their fifties or early sixties, some of them with women hanging on their arms like accessories.

"Gives a new meaning to the term manbag." This catty thought is expressed in Fae's voice

"Love's complexion has many hues," I immediately self-edit. Luckily, Colin is still staring into his pint.

There is a definite dress code, baggy and nonbinary. Trainers, flared jeans, and extra large T-shirts with tattoo designs or slogans on the front, and often down the long sleeves too. Images, like body paint, which will animate in movement on the dance floor. Some of the T-shirts are literally holy relics, bought in Affleck's Palace decades ago. I recognise the straplines, 'ON THE SIXTH DAY GOD CREATED MANchester and 'Woodstock 69, Manchester 89.' Northern pride, Northern attitude. The men that still have any hair sport mop-tops, those that don't wear bucket hats or flat caps on their heads. The women have shoulder length floppy hair, hung centre-parted like curtains.

The sound of guitars being tuned announces imminent activity. The stage is a low construction made from wooden pallets, bound together by hope and coach bolts. The four male musicians are indistinguishable from their audience, members of the same cult. The band don't introduce themselves. Their music says everything anyone needs to know about them and the ambience of the evening: love, freedom, and happiness. It flows like an elixir with ingredients of acid house,1960s pop, and psychedelia melting into rainbow ribbons of sound, entrancing the crowd into loose limbed dance. Soon the room is engulfed with rhythmic waves of movement, an ocean of swaying humanity. I can smell the musky aroma of heat generated by people, sweetened by a scent of warm weed which drifts like incense. I let the music massage my body, connected by sound and sensation to the men and women around me. It's a kind of collective worship, a renewal of belief in better worlds. I beckon Colin to join me, but only his eyes move across the dancefloor, stalking me with a blue intensity I find embarrassing. He makes me aware of individual shape, beaching me beyond the tide of wellbeing swelling the room.

I don't sense the approaching storm, can't see the sky bruising. The hammering of the thunder, rumbling like barrels rolling over cellar stone flags, is drowned in the music. Electricity splinters, cracks whips of jagged white light with neon blue tendrils above the venue but its rage is ignored until a bolt forks and fuses the lights and amps. The silence is momentarily louder than the thunder. The band and dancers are suspended in freeze-frame. Then the static scene strobes into slow motion.

"Sorry party people, but that's the end of the gig. Lightning never strikes in the same place twice so we'll reschedule for next week. Your tickets will still be valid." Mick is calm but emphatic. "Luckily no one seems hurt, but please can you leave as soon as possible."

The band begin to check themselves and their instruments for signs of damage as people grope about, draining glasses and looking for coats. Mick opens the doors wide and rain is falling like a drum roll at the threshold. The pub empties quickly. Colin watches me help Mick collect glasses and sips his pint slowly as the band pack up hurriedly.

"We'll be off then Mick," the lead guitarist is hovering.

"Okay mate, thanks for tonight," Mick hands him a roll of notes secured with a rubber band. "Good job you're travelling west, the bridge at Callis is properly flooded."

Colin looks at me, jiggles his house keys in his fingers before silencing them in his fist; "I don't want you to risk flooded roads. You could stay at mine tonight, better safe than sorry." He senses my hesitation but ignores it. "Thanks Mick, great gig, apart from the power issue. Come on Alice, it's only a five minute walk." Colin strides out of the open door and I have to run to catch up with him.

The rain is horizontal now and smarts our faces as we walk up a slippery stone- flagged path. An owl hoots, hunting prey or a mate. A Victorian mill owner's mansion looms out of the darkness. Colin sprints into the porch, steadies himself against one of the pillars and shakes himself. I follow like a goose behind him.

"My flat's on the ground floor, so the dogs can access the back garden," Colin shouts over frenzied barking as he turns the key in the large wooden door. It opens wide like a warm mouth. We enter into a grand hallway, decorated with an embossed wallpaper of entwining leaves in several shades of green. The broad cornice is painted brown and is textured with plaster depictions of hazelnuts, acorns, and sweet chestnuts. A graceful wrought-iron staircase sweeps upwards like a curving wave. It is shielded by a tall ornate gate, patterned by elaborate metal scrolls and finials.

"This way," Colin disappears through a glossy white door to the right.

We leave the deciduous décor of the hallway and step into tropical rainforest. Banana and cinchona trees, bamboo and palms have been painted with an artist's brush on the walls. Orchids and passion flowers bloom on the tall skirting boards. The furniture is antique and elegant, carved from mahogany and rosewood. A flock of crafted birds, made from felt and feather, perches on top of the marble fireplace. Their black eyes are opaque. A lagoon of blue carpet softens the polished floor-boards in the centre of the room.

"It's gorgeous. Sumptuous." I try to imagine what it would be like to clean a place like this.

"You haven't seen it all yet." Colin orders the dogs back into their beds, then slips into estate agent mode as he reveals the kitchen's granite worktops, gold taps and ebony cabinets.

"I'm saving the best bit until last," he announces as he opens the bedroom door with a flourish. An enormous bed with a grass-green quilt forms an island in an ocean of blue-grey walls. Sea horses and angel fish swim around the cornice in carefully brushed colours, sandy-brown, pale orange, blue and yellow. The ensuite is a spa, shining silver. It gleams like wave-washed pebbles.

"Poseidon's horse will ride high on the tide tonight." Fae's voice emerges from the caves of my mind, "Love is always the breaker," she says with glee, "rolling us out into unfathomable sea."

Noticing for the first time since we entered the house that our clothes are dripping, I shiver. To avoid looking directly at Colin, I explore the room with my eyes and discover a glass display case on a large bedside table. Inside is a grotesque, life size papier mâché bust of a woman. She has a ghastly pallor. Her face is crazed with wrinkles beneath a shock of platinum blonde hair. The jugular vein on her neck is distended, bloodshot eyes bulge and the full lips pout. Her nipples are hard and protruding.

"Oh, that's the wife," Colin's breath, hot and malty on the back of my neck, startles me. He flips his hand dismissively in the direction of the sculpture. "Ex-wife now, of course. Thought of herself as an artist. It's a self-portrait".

I stare at the artwork. The artist has signed her name in bold letters, Sue Hill.

"Hill, so is that your surname?"

"Yes and the witch still calls herself Mrs. And do you know the bitch wanted it back when she took off. But it was a gift, and you can never take back what you've given."

"I have given you nothing, nothing of me, do you hear," I shout. "Forget you ever met me, forget all about me, where I live, even my name."

"Come on, don't be like that, Sue."

I can tell by his smirk that this isn't a slip of the tongue, but a fatuous attempt at humour.

"I have enough trouble remembering who I am without people messing with my head. Leave me alone."

I flee, running through the forest hallway. I slam the heavy front door shut, blocking out the baying of the dogs, muting the voices.

That night, back at home, I sleep fitfully. I dream of a fair, in a field of trampled grass. Creatures with clown faces and cobweb masks stroll between striped tents. Their cloaks with drags of fringe and fur swirl as they walk towards me. Fae and Colin are amongst them. My phone shatters in my hand and broken glass shimmers on the ground. Panic rises in a crescendo of discordant notes.

As soon as it's light I visit my listening tree, but only for a silent hug.

I do not respond to any future approaches from Colin. Neither do I acknowledge Fae's comments about the whole affair, "You can't control the flow, stop the ebb, untangle the web."

She repeats the words over and over in my head, but each time her voice is fainter, "You can't control the flow, stop the ebb, untangle the web" until it fades, inaudible. Eventually she too fades, an insubstantial shadow. Finally, I realise what strength I have is my own. Comfortable in my skin, I breathe free like the sea.

The Medicinal Garden

The garden is thriving, but I am not. My whole world in five square metres of sloping ground, in three raised beds, in one corolla of a single flower. The colour and positioning of every plant proclaims my right to choose. I sit on an old wooden bench as weathered as my face; my hands eager to take hold of a warm, soothing cup of herbal tea. But not yet, not just yet.

First I need to drink-in the colour of this gathering sunset. The daffodils' golden trumpets have finished their fanfare, but their brassy memory remains. Hellebores are fading gracefully, drooping curved petals like the hems of modest petticoats. Their faces maintain only the palest of pink blushes. Foxgloves are dark-green rosettes, pinned proudly onto the soil. They will soon shoot tall and straight, unfurling purple fairy hats. Oval emerald leaves, fashioned with a neat trim and elegant tailored point, bristle on the hydrangea; clothed in anticipation of a glorious host of late summer blooms. The fresh-scenting of white evening primrose tempts me to stay awhile.

The hospital had smelt of clinical professionalism and overcooked vegetables. I was directed down sterile corridors towards the monstrous bulk of the MRI scanner.

A nurse asked me to take off my wedding ring, the amber necklace I always wore, and my watch. As the key turned in the regulation metal locker, my personal effects categorised and stored, I felt my personality haemorrhage.

Slotted horizontally into the MRI tube, I was trapped and tinned. The radiographer's words were muffled by my ear protection, which failed to soften the screaming bleeps of the machine. Finally, it regurgitated me. I was led into a small room and told to wait for the consultant.

"It's positive," he said, a voluminous white coat making him look like a fancy-dress ghost. A spark of joy cremated into ash as I realised he meant positive in a medical sense. The consultant's voice continued in a sympathetic tone, but his words floated above me and I could not give them substance … "we can't cure terminal illness, but we can alleviate the symptoms." He smiled at me as if I were a child with a cold.

In the garden only the oleander is a constant companion, ever green. The leaves are lance shaped, a guard of honour for the funnels of red blossom which will flourish later in the year. I do not think I can wait that long to witness their splendour. I know that there is only one way to relieve my symptoms. I understand there is only one person who can do that.

I snip a few leaves from the oleander shrub with a pair of sharp secateurs and switch the kitchen kettle on.

The Repair Café

Even my kite couldn't raise my mood this morning, couldn't take me high. It lay like an injured mythological bird, downed by disbelief, colours flapping on the muddy football pitch. Fabric wings mangled by a cutting wind; cords knotted and the plastic crossbar bent like a boomerang.

The park is desolate on this February afternoon. The café is closed, shuttered against the cold, and the skateboard area is deserted. A couple of bored dog walkers lead their listless hounds around circular paths with no destination. My numb hands delve into my pockets, searching for gloves I don't expect to find.

"Have you lost something?" I'm startled by the sudden appearance of the woman beside me.

"No. Well yes, but only the expectation of flight." My laugh is not convincing and the woman doesn't smile. She cocks her head and stares directly at me. I see my reflection in the black pupils of her bird-like eyes.

"You need the Repair Café," she says. "There's a poster on the Co-op community noticeboard; the why, when, and where of it all scheduled."

By the time I finish gathering the limp, broken kite into a black bin liner, the woman has vanished.

In contrast to the park, the supermarket hums with activity; the electric drone of freezer cabinets, the harsh flickering of a faulty fluorescent light strip, and the anxious scouring of reduced-price shelves by customers clutching their mobile phones like talismans against rising costs. I ignore the brightly coloured plastic packages with their false promises of hearty food and scan the noticeboard. It is reassuringly old fashioned. Handwritten posters, imploring or enticing, are pinned at ungainly angles like arms in an awkward hug.

The Repair Café advert pledges "help, advice and assisted repairs with skilled volunteers," as well as "tea, coffee and homemade cakes." I could definitely "come for a cuppa and see what it's like." Eating cake at ten o'clock in the morning would be the most hedonistic activity I'd indulged in for years.

The kite sags in its body bag on my kitchen floor for several days before I swing it over my shoulder in firefighter style and march up the steep stone setts to Heptonstall. The village grips the hilltop, bound to its footings only by the weight of history and a tangle of tree roots. I am balancing on a precipice and enter the Victorian school hall with small, uncertain steps.

The elderly man at reception regards me solemnly, his long grey beard gesticulating like a third hand as he speaks, "Have you been here before? If not, you'll have to fill out a form and read the rules. Bloody bureaucracy, but it will only take two minutes."

"That's at least 120 to 200 heartbeats, possibly more because you've just climbed the hill." I recognise the interjecting voice immediately. It is the woman from the park, her eyes crinkling years of mischief. She looks even slighter in the full-length green velvet dress she is wearing; she had been hunkered down in a heavy coat when I first encountered her.

"Hello Sophia. Shouldn't you be brewing." The beard points to a large urn which is steaming noisily in the corner of the room.

"Come on, I'll make you a cup of tea."

As Sophia beckons me, her fingers conducting currents of warm air, I gather up the required paperwork. Dutifully, I read the rules, which announce their importance in ornate italic print at the top of the form. 'Wherever possible, visitors to the café carry out the repairs themselves, at their own risk, with guidance from our expert volunteers. We do not accept any liability for consequential damage or loss of any kind resulting from the advice or help freely given at the Repair Café.'

The scent curling from the ochre-red infusion Sophia places next to my right hand soothes with base notes of Autumn woodland and encourages me to start completing the form.

It begins conventionally enough,

"Name and contact details?"

Soon becoming stranger with,

"Star sign?"'

"Please select the word that best describes your mood this morning: bright, dark, cloudy, misty, other."

"Please place a tick alongside the beings you believe in; gods, the devil, demons, dragons, faeries, witches, wizards, ghosts, giants, grindylows, mermaids, selkies, boggarts, hobbits .....' The list seems endless.

"You don't have to fill it all in, we're not a government agency. Just make sure you sign at the bottom that you've read and understood the rules." Sophia's pragmatism cheers me. I don't have to be perplexed by events, I don't need to try and puzzle out the meaning of everything, all the time.

"Just experience it," advises Sophia. "Especially this cherry cake, it will cheer you up." The cake does indeed sustain me, light and sweet, shot with ripe fruit. Sophia waits until I have cleared the wisteria-patterned plate of every crumb with my index finger before she looks at the parcel containing my kite, which lies like a black shadow behind my chair.

"Your kite isn't dead. We need to take it out of that bin-liner and let it breathe." Sophia transports the slippery package onto one of the tables that hem the sides of the hall like neat stitches. Behind these stalls sit the repair experts, the tools of their trade laid out before them.

My kite is placed beside a sewing machine, a pair of pliers, two sets of scissors, an anthology of comic poems, and a pin cushion hedgehog; quilled with shining needles. A young person with long auburn hair is perched on a stool beside the table.

"Hi, I'm Althea, your repair buddy. We don't see anything as rubbish, everything, everybody is repairable."

"It just fell from the sky," I say.

"Like you?" Althea asks gently.

"It's days since we argued in the pub," I blurt. "On the way home we crossed a bridge, kissed goodbye, but he tasted bitter. He strode away quickly and I haven't seen him since."

"Turbulent waters," Althea counsels, "ambered by peat. Now you are alone, listening to the calls of the night."

"Not quite alone," I say. "My husband still lives with me. He doesn't suspect."

Althea spreads the wings of the kite gently, surveying the damage. "You hide behind the fan of your feathers. You're lucky it didn't rip right down the middle."

"It's me that's cut in two," I exclaim, then wonder why I'm confiding in this stranger.

"Will you be able to sew it together again? I hope Althea will focus on my questions, forgetting my earlier outburst. "Is the waterproof cloth too thick for your sewing machine?"

"We can sew anything, but not always seamlessly," Althea speaks with a quiet confidence. "We darn material, stitch lives, mend gaping holes. We leave the repair of broken bodies to doctors, but we can fix fractured hearts."

Althea places the torn kite beneath the needle of the sewing machine and an electronic beat penetrates her speech.

"My colleague reconditioned a broken vacuum cleaner last week," Althea stares directly at me, all the while feeding the fabric through the needle clamp of a sewing machine. "There were tangled strings of hair around the brushes. The client was afraid of unclipping the motor head to empty the dust canister, which was full to bursting. You see, she had vacuumed her husband up, perhaps by mistake, she wasn't sure. He had never offered to help her clean. He would sit, eyes fixed on his phone. The only acknowledgement of her labour, of her very existence, would be to lift his legs a few inches above the carpet when she was hoovering beneath them. She'd seen his body flatten, feet first, then slowly disappear with the force of the suction."

"Was the woman able to use the vacuum cleaner again?" I ask.

"She chose not to," Althea answers. "She was afraid he might be released, either as a cloud or in person, like a genie from a bottle, not granting wishes but bestowing curses, so she donated it to the charity shop near the town hall and switched to a broom instead; less environmental impact, and anyway now her husband has gone there's less dust about the house. Here, take the end of this cord. Together we'll untwist the ropes, undo the knots, release the tension."

And so the unravelling begins. Althea's fingers dancing nimbly along the control line; mine initially clumsy but soon disentangling the harness. Althea hums a patchwork of songs I half remember. I find myself joining in, a forgotten rhythm of happiness in my head. I uncoil with the kite's ropes.

"It's complete." Althea announces suddenly, eyes glittering stars.

"It's wonderful, perfectly restored."

"Take your kite to where the moorland meets imagination; chase your visions across wide horizons and fly your dreams."

And that's exactly what I intend to do, but only after I've been to that charity shop.

House of Straw

Before you read my story and judge me, I want to ask a question. How many personas have you play-acted over the years; how many layers of life lie in you like rock strata?

"It's time for the pig to hit the deck," Mr. Pickles had decreed. My stomach fluttered, the way it used to when I was hungry before my evacuation to the farm. I knew pig wasn't a pet. He only had one purpose in life. Butchery was his destiny.

I was fond of the pig and feeding him was my favourite job. Pig had accepted me with calm complacency, exploring the hands that brought his bucket of food each morning with a moist snout. His skin was warm with hairs that ruffled when I stroked him. Such human skin, freckled like my dad's upper arms when he had cradled me as a baby.

Pig's physicality and the pleasure it had given me, was in stark contrast to the hostility of the hens. Sharp beaks blooded my fingers as I groped for the smooth eggs beneath their foul bodies. They talked rebellion in clucking dialogue which turned into a cackling crescendo every time I pulled back the screeching bolt of the henhouse door.

It had all begun with a train ride. Departure 1940, fleeing an aerial bombardment that hadn't yet begun, except in the imagination of worried parents who saw burning buildings and dying relatives whenever they closed their tired eyes. As my mother was so fond of saying, you never know what's down the track. Only sometimes you did know. Maybe not scary specifics, but a suspicion you'd end up somewhere you wouldn't choose to be. I didn't hear all of my mother's parting words, they were muted by the train snorting steam into the gloom. We hugged goodbye. Another angular shape in the confused tangle of embracing bodies on a crowded platform.

It had been a damp, dispiriting journey. I can still remember the stale smell of childhood urine and fear. I can still see the small, pale faces, pocked by crumbs from packed lunches and streaked with tears. I did not cry.

On arrival we were herded into a cavernous village hall for selection by host adults, who studied us as if they were buying stock at a cattle market. The tallest of the older boys were picked out first, then the younger girls. Mr. and Mrs. Pickles selected me from the group of evacuees just as I was beginning to feel abandoned.

"We've brought the Fordson, lass, you're lucky, it's a long walk," Mr. Pickles grinned at me, a cheerfulness I could not respond to. I expected a bright red tractor, like in the storybooks, but disappointingly it was dark green.

Now I know life isn't painted in primary school colours, isn't as simple as secondary school mathematics with absolute values and rules. One plus one may not equal two. In my experience one plus one made three. All these decades later "my husband's" wife still walks beside me with a particular gait, a specific scent, a silent accusation.

Mrs. Pickles and I were loaded into a trailer, which still contained strands of straw, before Mr. Pickles climbed into the single seat of the tractor. There was a strong smell of diesel as we chugged through the village and then onto a steep cobbled incline. The Pickles' stone farmhouse was shrouded in hills, a moorland landscape etched into their faces. Dark circles like sunken peat had settled beneath their eyes, features sculptured by water and wind.

At the farm routine rode with nature, the cycles of light and darkness. Seasons stained my hands. In spring they were brown, caked with mud. Palms flecked yellow with pollen in summer, before staining blackberry-purple in autumn. During the winter they were blue with sharp cold.

"There's them that's on rations and there's them that's on rashers," Mr. Pickles often said with an exaggerated wink. The buckets of scraps I had hauled across the yard for weeks had all been the messy means to an end.

Pig looked up inquisitively when Mr. Pickles appeared in an oilskin overall. Mr. Pickles gestured that I should come out of the pen and handed me a bright yellow rubber apron and black galoshes.

"Put these on please, Elizabeth. Then fetch the baking bowl from the kitchen."

Mrs. Pickles waddled into the yard similarly attired. As if at some peculiar picnic, she spread a tarpaulin over the cobbles and placed soap, scrubbing brushes, a small saw, and several knives upon it.

"Here," Mr. Pickles handed me an acorn. "Hold it through the bars, lass. Don't move." Pig looked directly into my eyes. I stroked his soft ears, tracing the web of red veins threading beneath the plush pink velvet. He extended his wrinkling snout towards the acorn. I smelled the living softness of Pig and the stiff rubber stench of Mr. Pickles' bulk, kneeling as if in prayer beside me, before he slowly raised his arm and tensed his hand. The gun barrel hovered like a bluebottle between the animal's eyes.

Pig shrieked as the shot exploded. I remember stumbling sideways, my gaze transfixed with slaughter as Mr. Pickles winched Pig up, steadying his swinging in a gruesome embrace, and slit his throat. Blood spewed out, splashing into the bowl Mr. Pickles held like an offering before a god.

"We need to bathe the meat," said Mrs. Pickles. Pig had metamorphosed into meat, the difference between life and death, an animal without animation. Three little pigs, only this one didn't need a house anymore and the wolves were walking on two legs.

All three of us began to scrub the skin. Hair, blood and mud mixing, forming tributaries running over the pig's flanks. There was a smell of sweat, of rusting iron, and death not yet putrefied by decay.

Pig looked vulnerable, an unclothed kind of clean, before Mr. Pickles inserted a large knife into its anus, separating the skin like a prophet parting the waves of a rippling sea; exposing pale fat and muscle beds.

The coiled guts unravelled and drooped like a twisted rope, sagging with gravity. Mr. Pickles carefully cut them loose, so as not to damage the vital organs, and they tumbled like tresses of demon hair onto the ground. His fingers traced the shape of the liver, heart and lungs, loosening the wrapping of tissue delicately, before prising them out of the carcass.

Panting with exertion, Mr. Pickles then sawed at the pig's flabby neck, his grunts rasping into the sound of metal grating on bone. The huge head landed with a deep drum beat before bouncing like a ball in a grotesque game; finally settling beside the severed cloven hooves which looked like the devil at play had discarded them.

They say only the good die young. I look at my birthday cards, ninety-five in glittering numerals shines on them - only I'm not. I'm ninety. Old enough to know some secrets cannot be shared. They need to be stored, airtight, to stop the mould, to stem the spores creeping across your sleep.

At first I had worn my new identity like a glamorous grown-up dress but then it became familiar as an old frock. He had suggested it, standing tall and handsome in his blue R.A.F. uniform, a shaft of sunlight illuminating his head like the cheap icon in my boarding-house room. The debris of the night before was scattered on the twisted sheets of the sagging bed, the precious pair of nylons snaking like a skinned eel on top of it.

It was 1946. Identities and ideas were churning, blasted like shrapnel, shattering the old structures of society. Replacing my ration card had been easy. So many papers, so many people, had disintegrated into dust and ashes in burning homes. I didn't at all mind being five years older at the stroke of an official pen. It was important that I appeared to be of an age that made our marriage believable. And he was right, his wife would never agree to divorce him.

He asked me to accompany him home after his demobilisation. We walked along a steep, dark pavement lined with trees made skeletal by winter, not war. The graceful Victorian villas with their ornate facades were mostly intact, except for the end terrace which gaped open, a loose jagged jaw. Bricks like discarded teeth were scattered across the garden. Shredded curtains flapped forlornly; white flags from smashed windows.

His key opened the lock on the imposing front door of number four. His wife appeared ethereal in a flimsy dressing gown on the landing as he leapt up the sweeping staircase. His hands gliding above, but not quite touching, the handrail.

I watched in the wings of the hallway as he encircled his wife in his arms, waltzing as if at the dancehall, moving to imaginary music. Him whirling her towards the stairs. A toy ballerina turning on the top of a jewellery box. She pirouetted for a second and plummeted. Then she was just a crumple of clothes right there in front of me, motionless. It was an execution. Another of the countless casualties of wartime, but unlike the pig there was no higher purpose, no prospect of forgiveness.

"Help me," he grunted, as he dragged the bundle, sprawled like a splattered insect, away from the bottom step. His glazed eyes avoided mine. I recoiled as he thrust the horrific, inert fingers towards me. Five hands in an inhuman clasp; to have and to hold, binding. We wrestled with his wife's wedding ring, the hairs on his knuckles glistening with perspiration. Eight living fingers writhing and twisting until the ring reluctantly released its grip and clattered onto the floor.

We buried his wife immediately in the rubble of the bombed-out house on the street corner. Nobody passed us as he carried the body, contorted into his large kit bag, across his shoulders in the depth of the night.

No suspicions or accusations have ever surfaced from the turmoil of post war reconstruction. I have inherited a wedding ring, two names, two birthdays, and a lifetime of lying.

Confluence

It was me, but it wasn't me. This familiar face staring back, unblinking, from a pool deep green in reflected woodland. A place petrified in stone, chiselled by the breaking-in of a beck. The straining of sinews to do the relentless bidding of an industrial revolution that left a valley scarred and charred. Above the treeline the Pennines loom black, a crow's head silhouette. The crag beak is pointed, the hillsides feathered with heathery quills.

The sun is a glossy eye, harsh and penetrating. The light intensifies, pulsating like an electronic screen. Though I doubt there is a signal my fingers check the phone is in my pocket, the way I used to reach for a cigarette. Habitual impulses, muscles flexing without conscious thought.

The art gallery yesterday didn't conjure other worlds for me, as it usually did. I had been fascinated by a model of a small black bear, but the artist blocked my gaze.

"Made from wax and human hair," she said proudly. I wondered if she stuck pins into it, or ravens' plumes, because this is what I want to do to you. As our magic weakens, I wish to strengthen my waning powers, wash out your scent with carbolic soap, by the ringing of cloth and hands.

You sauntered around the gallery before stopping to scoff at an illustration of a "male womb," alongside a stylised figure of a man and a single feather from a peacock's tail, the eyespots staring, unseeing, in brilliant blue and bright turquoise.

"I'm exploring the connection between fatherhood and creativity," the artist said bravely. I didn't ask if he'd ever gnawed through an umbilical cord or even smelt the birth blood.

I am finding it hard to cut the lifeline that holds me to you. Bound together we flail among the waves, pulling each other off balance.

This wild water swimming will calm me, freeze my thoughts. The face blurs in a disturbance of flies above the water. A breeze furrows lines, sets the lips thinner, quarries the nose sharper. If I'm going to take a dip, I need to do it quickly. Embrace the thrilling cold, let the shock burst, the adrenalin pulse.

The pebbles beneath my feet are slipper smooth for the first few steps and then scissor sharp. Icy immersion stiffens every hair on my body, pumps my breath into rapid gasps. My legs are frog, arms the bow of a boat, the stillness in front of me becoming waves in my wake. My body is alive, every nerve singing falsetto. I understand the meaning of the word cold, a startling comprehension. I do not understand the word love, but it no longer matters in this buoyant state that appears to be without gravity.

The pool looks and feels like a coconut truffle, dark and rippling, flecked with fine white blossom. In the centre the tips of my toes sink into rich praline silt. Under water, my limbs are shimmering gold in peat-reflected light.

Towards the waterfall, just beyond the pool, the river rushes across an old mill race and air bubbles surface as if a subterranean creature sleeps below. Breathing heavily it is undisturbed by the aquatic insects that skim above: black water striders, their long legs skating, brown water boatmen paddling frantically and stonefly flashing orange from their wings. Floating on my back, I hear the great wooden mill wheel, long since rotted, revolving, whirring faster than the hovering mayflies.

The afternoon is turning towards evening and a chilly wind stirs me to clamber out of the beck. There is a strong smell of water mint and I glimpse its tiny purple flowers peering shyly from behind razored stones. My skin is goose pimpled as I towel myself dry vigorously and push shivering limbs into clothes which feel shrunk and awkward.

I scramble onto the steep bank, grasping tough clumps of coarse grass to help me ascend. The plentiful Hemp Agrimony, or Holy Rope, won't hold my weight. Its stalks of mauve flowers threaded like rosary beads are fragile.

"May your bathing be a baptism." A woman looms over me as I haul myself up from my knees. I recognise her from the reflection in the pool.

"Thank you." I stammer, not sure what else to say and noticing with alarm that she is carrying a hammer.

"I'm the sculptor of the crags and outcrops," the woman says, aware of me looking warily at the hammer. She points to a large wicker basket full of boulders next to her on the footpath.

"I created the Bridestones and the Old Woman Stones. I am both Brigid, the goddess, and Cailleach, the witch. We are not rivals; we are two sides of the same glittering coin. We balance light and darkness, warmth and cold. Love and hate, of self and others. We work in harmony. Recognise our faces, we both live within you. Spend the wealth of experience we gift you wisely. "

I promised myself under the celestial canopy of ancient trees to try and do just that.

Part Three - Expelled from Happy Valley

The Edit

Your hands haunt me
one curving a soft fist
freckled with fine hair
one holding a pen
following printed lines
of words paragraphed
by coffee and comment.
My thoughts naked
before your eyes.

My fingers uncurling.
An ache to touch
as red ink bleeds
onto the pages
of a stained story.

Hare-brained

I watch, eastwards
in mercury moonshine
the lightfoot looms
ears like split purses
casting silver lore
across fields to seed.
Eyes peat amber
wells into wisdom.
Windswift messenger
shallow hiding in hollows.
Sighting you is a covenant
renewed, not broken.

Cross Bay Walk

A careless horizon
frames sand palettes
beige to brown
in darkening stripes.
Placid in glistening haze
belying signs of 'Danger.'

A path marked
by myrtle branches
thrust into shoreline flesh.
A long line of people
flotsam dots
black silhouettes
in a dazzle of heat.
Two tractors
harvesting dreams.

Only the hard ridges
of wet mud ripples
suggest a tide retreated.
Ideas sink in sand
evaporate as foam
swallowed by rising water.
Words are washed empty

stranded creatures
in rock pools of poetry.

Channel currents tug
a resurgence, flowing
sentences like shanties.
Trapped in deep ebb
I wade through stars
sparking an ocean.

Shadow Puppeteer

In a theatre of drawn expectation
her choreographed fingers
weave air
wax shadow
curate shade.
Our darkness flashes
as clapping hands
catch the light like fish-scales.

Nightjar

She watches the Harvest Moon
lantern glinting on blown apples
gleaming like Christmas baubles
on a dark deciduous tree.

Stark branches still festooned
in garlands of russet yellow
apple dipping for night birds
during speckled dusk.

Drunk plump on fermenting
fruit and preserved insects
in fat duvet feathers
they perch hunched.

Opening the casement wide
she drinks a champagne of stars
silhouetted in a bedroom window
behind the half-drawn curtains of her life.

Haworth Moor

The wind flings words here-
they braid stalks of grass
flutter papery leaves
glide the fustian moor.

The beck sings words here-
they are bit by ice
spat by torrential rain
shredded dry in sun.

The stone seeps words here-
they are hewn from rock
carved by millstone grit
particles of the dead.

The words settle here-
they are crows perching
curlews circling sky
moss spores weaving poetry.

Dementia Ward

The nurses are delivering,
not babies but medical supplies
blank plastic boxes
holding confusing contents.

Barbara, in the bed opposite
sees airline snacks on a plane
"It's on me, I'll pay," she shouts
as the trolley trundles past.

At the ward corner, Joyce
plays discordant ragtime jazz,
her body music
conducting the monitors.

Mum has bad news
Dad's grandad has just died
and she can't remember
the menu for a funeral tea.

Patients like benign banshees
glide across the floor
NHS nighties billowing
on toilet transport.

Sometimes it's a car wash
showers from shivering hoses.
Then a noisy circus
with rows of curtain tents.

A chair's echoing scrape
is the cry of escaped elephants.
"Quiet as you leave,
cats sleep in the corridors."

The satnav says drive straight ahead,
I'm all at sea
capsizing under a low sky
tasting salt water.

Ode to a Clay Pipe

Smooth in barnacled hands
clay moulded from heavy earth
bone dry, like a hare's femur
bleached skeletal.
I inhale you
between the breathing of peat
and the rasping of sandstone.
Chamber glowing acrid
heather burnt to black stalks.
Lips a wound opening
sucking a bitter strand.
Pipe dreams ascending
in fleeces of smoke.

They and Them

When do ideas become ideology?
From the drawing room
to drawing up distinctions
ink lines on a map
ink stamped onto papers
tattooed into a human arm.

The binding of thought
shackling of knowledge
cutting of connections.
The plotting of people on graphs
classified by dots of a certain colour
just 'not us.'

My Matinee Idol

Your hands were large
warm and strong
my child fingers
nested in their comfort.

The shining parts
of your profession
were cold and small
tiny screws of thought.

You worked in miniature
Cogs and levers and keys
to the chatter of typewriters
the tapping of adding machines.

The heavy wonder of metal cases
with intricate oiled insides
their accuracy and speed
matching your mechanic's skill.

Child Cargo

I churn like the sea
swimming ice water shock
for Rose Alice and me.

A child's tears swelling
cheeks salt-whipped, alone,
beset by fears.

Officially a *Waif and Stray*
transported for being poor
forced to migrate.

Clutching a bag full of charity
you left without a chance
to say goodbye to siblings.

No one gave a second glance
as you walked the gangplank
of Church and Empire.

From Liverpool to Quebec
HMS Canada crossed oceans
emotions breaking like waves.

Shipped by batch and number
designation servant, faraway
from the Humber, your estuary.

You never talked, Rose Alice,
about the time your Spring petals
were torn and cast into the sea.

Retirement

If I search will I spot you
beneath an upturned stone

toad squat
work worm still writhing

the old employed me
toil stained

brain blotched
eyes flickering, tongue twitching

haunches crouching discomfort
hunkered down

camouflaged dull grey
skin pummelled dry ?

Corked

In a browning hotel room
we taste the music of wine
notes smelling strongly of fruit
and faintly of leather.
We rise into a pink-flushed sky
before downing the sediment.
Our noses reach for a future
but the effervescence has elapsed.
Only tannin bitterness
is left of our bouquet.

Handmade Parade

Earth vibrates to snare drums.
We sit side saddle on a bench
resting arms on horses' heads.
Early afternoon sun smiles
at the colourful gathering crowd.
Humans attached by leads
to dogs in jackets and neckties.
Dryads walk in procession
leafy garland hair swaying.
Stick insect people dance on stilts.
Fish on flagpoles swim the air.
A bull with highland horns trots
in taffeta kilt of many colours.
Fox plays without fear of hounds
badgers frolic outside their sets.
A giant white goose pecks
with a huge orange beak
and a golden egg is laid.
Creatures born of magic and misrule
formed by imagination,
wire and wishful-thinking.
The sorcery of cardboard and of paint.

The Prophesy

I lay on stone slabs
beating heart
beneath
a parasol of Autumn trees.

I close my eyes
you radiate
intense
a pure white light.

I breathe with moss
leafblown kisses
falling
reddening my lips.

Abandoned - revisiting a former art gallery

The splintered bare bones of it
bleached white - chalk dust grief
tasting of dry blanched almonds.

A stately mansion bequeathed
public gallery soon to be private flats.
Your architecture of love, oak framed.

You recall the elegant spire -
dovetailed scales ascending
into an egg-shell sky.

Neck of a mythological creature
stretching your church of memory
drifting yellow blown daffodils.

Petals collage verdant grass
where you dad, and mum, both sat.
Double portrait - now still life.

Afternoon tea - brewed light and sweet
amid water colour landscapes.
Reminiscence swirling rich oils.

Your chorus song of colour
from the brush strokes of tulips
ever silent - trodden underfoot.

Mirror Image

Outside the poem
a face smiles for others
cameo profile
sketch lines of experience
crinkling years with a sigh.

Inside the poem
self portrait in oils
full-frontal abstract
vibrant swirls of colour
escape a canvas stretched tight.

Worry Bearer

You gave me worry dolls.
Five cloth finger puppets
in the bright colours
of central America
verdant green, sun yellow
heart-blood red.

Their blackdash eyes
stitched on blank faces
show suffering without sight
witness abuse without sense.
Tiny, troubled bodies
absorbing stress.

A helping hand you say.
Stroke their tummies
put them under your pillow
they'll lift your heaviness
send you stillness
and sleep.

You do not say
the dolls are a substitute
a salve for loss

as you leave in the night
travelling solo, our map
silently folded.

Shower Block

Washing you
is like bathing an elephant
in the surgical light
of a cold winter dawn.

I was born of your body
but it is not now familiar.
Dust of decades has gathered
in our cracks and creases.

This corduroy skin suit
cannot contain your soul
its attempted escape rippling
from a creaking cage
of bone and cartilage.

The wrinkled shower hose knots
like a trunk and we remember
a blue plastic baby bath -
nappies surfacing like seals
in the boiling water of twin tubs.

Our role reversal embarrasses us
makes us mute with discomfort.
Though I am the eldest
we do not speak of such things.

The Terror - ghosts of Empire in Canada

A vehicle flashes metallic sun,
grinds along a narrow gravel road
scratching chalk through prairie.

Migrating geese fly in formation
clamouring for freedom
feathering a translucent blue sky.

She is happy in this land,
which sounds, smells, moves like sea,
tall grasses rolling in waves.

Her husband smiles at the wheel.
A universe of two – isolated, completes
the perfect circle of a harvest moon.

They imagine themselves pioneers
petrol tank full, compass poised
wilderness supplies stowed in the boot.

Conquerors too, confident in their right
to roam, to mould a foreign place
to fit their perceptions and desires.

Shorn fields of dry stalks,
huge rolled hay-balls scattered
like pieces from a giant's boardgame.

Handpainted billboard exhortations
"Be Grateful" and "Lead a Good Life."
Moose heads on warning signs.

A heavy truck ploughs past,
storming dust as it shudders
to a halt beside a small plaque.

'Lutheran School Historic Site.'
Two timber buildings, painted white
with brash red metallic roofs.

A cabin and a schoolhouse.
Earth humming and rustling
unfamiliar noises of unknown insects.

She crosses the threshold.
Desks filed in orderly rows, dead flies
dried grey, their wings torn paper.

A large commanding blackboard
"Kings and Queens of England,"
scrawled in spiky writing.

One sepia photograph
hangs from a single nail
a class of 'Metis' children.

Dark eyes stare from the frame
girls dressed in white pinafores
long hair clipped tightly to heads.

Boys wearing homespun tunics
hair cut short, military style
rigid bodies stood in line.

Beside them a fat man,
pink and hairy as a hog,
a rattan cane in his hand.

She hears her own breathing
a beating of blood, heavy sweat
below an acrid tang of fear.

On the back of her neck hairs spike,
sticky web spiders crawl
across her skin.

No figure forms in the silent shadows
but something malignant, monstrous

swells a sense of undiluted evil.

She freezes, stark, still,
bolts into sunshine, slams the door
behind her shut.

They continue driving to their destination
the milky river and saline plains.
She tastes only the salt of tears.

Soused

Left single, by myself
at night
brooding sky am I
cloud-mottled black
experience stained.

With you, us together
in daytime
azure blue am I
stroked sun yellow
love brushed.

We were shimmering silk
like the scarf
you bought me
before it rinsed grey
in the wash.

When stars dimmed
stopped threading
the space between us
becoming our prayer
beads of existence.

Drift

Snow steals depth from darkness
starches horizons white
blossoms frost on trees.
I remember the teeth-edge
grate of your shovel
scraping tarmac piebald.
The smell of powdered baby
in bleached morning light
as I watched
through a window
of cut glass ice.

Rhubarb

I party with rhubarb
arrived like a bunch of flowers
flecked stems blushing red
in a brown paper bouquet.
A gift of the gods, from a friend.
Decorations of curled taffeta
ribbons in lime green and pink
scatter the worktop surface
the swirling skirts of dancers.
An audience of fruit applauds.
Zesty excitement simmers
bubbles champagne laughter.
A jazz symphony of taste
tart, sweet aroma
fills my kitchen with joy.

Immersion - Van Gogh

We view from deck chairs
lovers in complementary hue
digital animation art.
Colours swirl vibrant.
A sun pulses molten orange
oscillating raw oriel.
Light rains pearls.
Almond blossoms float.

Spirals of emotion
spike in rich oils.
I am yellow
flooding a golden wheat field
where crows rise
black flags in storm skies.
A steam train approaches
fluent with an ending.

The Gift

Eostre's gift
is love bestowed
with free will.
This you have given me
a baptism of blue skies
pooling in your eyes.

In the ancestral hall
of my existence
white deer graze
in woven tapestries
their startled ears
flicking echoing fears.

On cloven turf
I offer you
my imperfect heart
trusting your full moon
will temper the tides
that threaten.

Sacred

Inside
your secret-garden shirt
and my wool layers clipped
from the backs of cloven beasts
heartbeats are blood berries
red as candied cherries
sighing in sweet cake.

Melody
an orchestra of thought
ripples the prayer pool
as we baptise newborn dreams
naked selves handfasting
shy emotion unmasking
our palms an offering.

Winter Afternoon

Love flutters softly
like leaves
mist ascends
a saturated valley
silent uncertainty seeps
wind rustles
thought congregations
birds roost
on graphite branches
your text flickers
and winter twilight
is liquid silver
heart alchemy

The Slug

I sense the stink of slug,
see grotesque slimy gloss
slowly unravelling, lengthening
a thick smear of piebald jelly.
Eel like, but without water
to give grace, it slides

Into consciousness
unseasonably early, flowers
just beginning to droop
bunting petals tattered.
On the hill behind my house
dusk blackens heather

Fetid tangs of Autumn
rise from mottled soil.
Quilted blackberries fall
with a soft sigh. Apples
ripen a faint blush
across waxy green skins.

There may yet be some sun
to surprise September
but still the slug is here,

worming into thought.
The therapist says
"The slug is a symbol."

I say, *It is real*
winding monstrous body
a serpent around the cat's bowl
in my kitchen. Always after dark
a mucous trail of eery glow.
Limacus Flavus.

"Avoidance," he says.
I look at him and say,
Do you have any idea
what it feels like
to stand on a slug
in your bare feet?

The Loosening

I lost your love
mislaid
like an old glove
worn
to the shape of my hand
ringed
with a wedding band
clasped
our fingers braided
unfold
emotions naked
unpicked
the marital bed
unmade
thread by thread.

Tidemark

Wind berates our house
slices the cry of gulls.
Tongues of spittle
lash dark windowpanes.
Rain beats a drum roll.
Anger drowns sleep.

This bed a ship sinking.
You a star fish stranded
on a shoreline of sheets.
In our wild winter
which should be summer
salty regret stings my lips.

Eye of the storm glints
swirls, constricts light.
A knot of misunderstanding
the flotsam of our past.
No lighthouse beam spans
the broiling sea between us.

Hoping our anchor holds firm
flailing, I release the rope
casting adrift

our umbilical cord
uncoiling a serpent
spiralling in perfect circles.

Radish

You blush crimson
as your bulb begins to swell
beneath the earth.

Embarrassed by your spice
in temperate climes
pushing light green leaves
modest frills of medicinal charm
above the soil shyly
disguising the sharp explosion
of a tongue of fire bite.

Cultivated in antiquity
depicted in fine drawings
decorating pyramid walls
a Chinese dynasties' delicacy
parting dark layers
an eastern sunset
within a pink veined globe.

You have a ripe wisdom
snow-crisp white flesh
flame heat in winter chill.

Reflection

If you were my best friend
I'd tell you to curate yellow
on bruised-black nights
when countless sheep
don't bring sleep.
Stop your wolf moon circling.
Hide exhibits
in your mind-museum of worry.

Paint by words,
brush light
into hollow doubt.
Fill fear with colour.
Sketch in thought lines.
Pick buttercups
from creases in curtains.

Depict Van Gogh
in sunflower blaze
but tear your gaze
from his gashed ear.
Surface yellow submarines
from dark depths.
Dance like the sea.

Picture blue tits
feeding on dreamcatchers.
Forsythia flowering
a ceiling canvas.
Design bright daffodils.
Watch their bonnets nod
because you cannot.

Tie yellow ribbons
on your bedpost
ready to welcome
the return of day.
Sing sharp piccalilli notes
fluting spices of turmeric
mustard and saffron.

Grin at smiling bananas
ripening a fruit bowl promise
of light to come.
Wait for the cracking of sky,
egg yolk sunrise
spreading like butter
on breakfast toast.

The Rising

She feeds a sourdough starter
froth breathes lung rhythms
sings a soprano of fermentation.

Flour puffs, sighs exhaustion
water and salt splatter, soothed
by unwinding ribbons of honey.

Stroking a thickening palette -
cloud colour, playing the artist
she has never become.

Moulding dough in envelope folds -
letters always meant to be sent
she has never posted.

Pressing a finger into loaves -
navels on the tummies of babies
she has never birthed.

Hours brew slowly
as dough rests and rises
swelling an aroma of summer fields.

Bread proves
living is not a recipe
it is an understanding.

By Their Fruits

A promise from summer
sweet blackberries ripening

Sparks of polka dot lightning
glint from bramble-bruised sky

Tightening green kernels
ebony beads clustered

Drupelets' soft kisses
brush upturned palms

Fingers stained scratched
pluck scents of burgundy

Quilt bodies purpling
bleed all around

Torn are the blood bonds
broken humanity

Ancient thorn covenant
crushed to the ground

War Drone

Cities overrun
deployment of missiles and men
citizens attacking tanks

we cannot verify

red stains of empire blotting maps
a devil riding horseback through Europe
limbs ripped from the living
flesh gouged still breathing
rats devouring the dead
horror in real time

we cannot verify

millions of refugees fleeing
names and numbers
lives packed in small suitcases

we cannot verify

lies are not truth
images are not fallout
the snow is not fake

dictatorship is not democracy
propaganda picking over the news
like the beak of a great carrion bird.

www.ingramcontent.com/pod-product-compliance
Lightning Source LLC
LaVergne TN
LVHW010059110826
845155LV00028B/412

* 9 7 8 1 9 1 6 5 1 1 0 6 4 *